The MISER on the MOUNTAIN

A NISQUALLY LEGEND OF MOUNT RAINIER

RETOLD BY

Nancy Luenn

ILLUSTRATIONS BY

Pierr Morgan

SASQUATCH BOOKS
SEATTLE

To Andrew and Taeko, with affection.
—N.L.

To Christine, Dennis and Ashley, Carole, Waldo, and Stefan,
for their generosity and love.
—P.M.

ACKNOWLEDGMENTS

The author would like to thank Cecelia Svinth Carpenter, Faith Hagenhofer,
and Jack McCloud for their generous assistance.
The illustrator wishes to thank Grace Ann Byrd at the Nisqually Tribal Library,
and Drew Crooks, curator of collections at the Washington State Capitol Museum in Olympia, Washington.

Published by Sasquatch Books
Distributed in Canada by Raincoast Books Ltd.

Printed in Hong Kong

Library of Congress Cataloging-in-Publication Data
Luenn, Nancy.
        Miser on the mountain : a Nisqually legend of Mount
Rainier / retold by Nancy Luenn ; illustrations by Pierr Morgan.
        p.   cm.
        Summary: Retells the traditional Pacific Northwest
Native American story of the man who climbs Mount Rainier to
collect a valuable shell and discovers what is important in life.
        ISBN 1-57061-082-7
        1. Nisqually Indians—Folklore. 2. Tales—Washington
(State) 3. Rainier, Mount (Wash.)—Folklore. [1. Nisqually Indians—
Folklore. 2. Indians of North America—Folklore. 3. Folklore—
Washington (State) 4. Rainier, Mount (Wash.)—Folklore.]
        I. Morgan, Pierr, ill. II. Title.
        E99.N74L84   1997
        398.2'089979—dc20 96-42392

Designed by Trina Stahl
Text set in Cloister Old Style
Display type set in Celestia Antiqua with Texas Hero
Illustrations executed in gouache and inks on Arches 140 pound
watercolor paper

SASQUATCH BOOKS
615 Second Avenue
Seattle, Washington 98104
(206) 467-4300
books@sasquatchbooks.com
http://www.sasquatch.com

Author's Note

THIS LEGEND IS PART of the oral tradition of the Nisqually
Indian Tribe. Legends like this one teach values: the right way to
live. Generosity and giving thanks are central to tribal life. The
miser's tale is told as an example of the wrong way to behave.

Hamitchou, the grandson of the miser, told Theodore
Winthrop his story in 1853. The first printed version appeared
in Winthrop's book *Canoe and Saddle* (Ticknor & Fields, Boston,
1862). Other retellings are found in *Indian Legends of the Pacific
Northwest,* by Ella E. Clark (University of California Press,
Berkeley, 1953), and in *Where the Waters Begin: The Traditional
Nisqually Indian History of Mount Rainier,* by Cecelia Svinth Carpenter
(Northwest Interpretive Association, Seattle, 1994).

The Nisqually Indian name for Mount Rainier is Ta-co-bet.
Traditional Nisqually believe the Great Mystery breathed a spirit
into every aspect of nature. They view the snowfields and glaciers
of Ta-co-bet as a sacred place, home of the spirits.

IN A VALLEY below the great mountain Ta-co-bet, there once lived a man named Latsut who loved *hiaqua*. He loved those barter shells, that *hiaqua*, more than anything else in his life. He filled baskets and boxes and caches with shells, but he still wanted more.

Latsut had a powerful totem, the elk. And so he was skilled as a hunter. His arrows flew straight, his fish spears were deadly, his food cache was full. Yet he never gave a feast as was the custom of his people.

"Feasting is wasteful," he said. "Those who feast will soon have empty bellies."

When others had emptied their caches, he traded dried meat for *hiaqua*.

Men called him miser—the one with clenched hands. Women said, "Greedy Latsut! He won't give his wife enough shells for a necklace!"

Latsut did not care what they said. He thought only of gathering treasure.

One day Latsut hunted an elk on the slopes of Ta-co-bet.
Bright snow on the mountainside dazzled his mind with a vision.
The elk he stalked turned. It spoke with the voice of the spirit.

Are you brave? asked Elk. *Do you dare seek my wealth that is hidden?*

"I dare," said Latsut. "I dare anything for *hiaqua!*"

Then listen, said Elk. *Climb great Ta-co-bet and learn the true meaning of wealth.*

Taut as the string of a bow, Latsut listened. *Seek for the lake at the summit. Find the three stones shaped like salmon, camas, and elk. Dig at the foot of your totem.*

The miser went home to prepare. He said nothing of where he was going. Only a crazy man climbed the white slopes of Ta-co-bet. Powerful spirits lived there.

He told his wife that he planned to go hunting. "Beca!" he said. "I need food for my journey. Go and dig camas."

While she was out in the meadow, Latsut carved two ice picks from elk horns. At sunset he filled a skin bag with dried fish and camas bulbs from his wife's basket. Then saying good-bye to his family, he set out to hunt for great wealth. He was much too impatient to wait until morning.

All night and the following day, Latsut moved along familiar forest paths. When night came again, he reached the cold edge of a snowfield. The night was too dark now to guide him. He huddled in what shelter he could find. Shivering, the miser dozed, afraid to light a fire that might beckon hostile spirits.

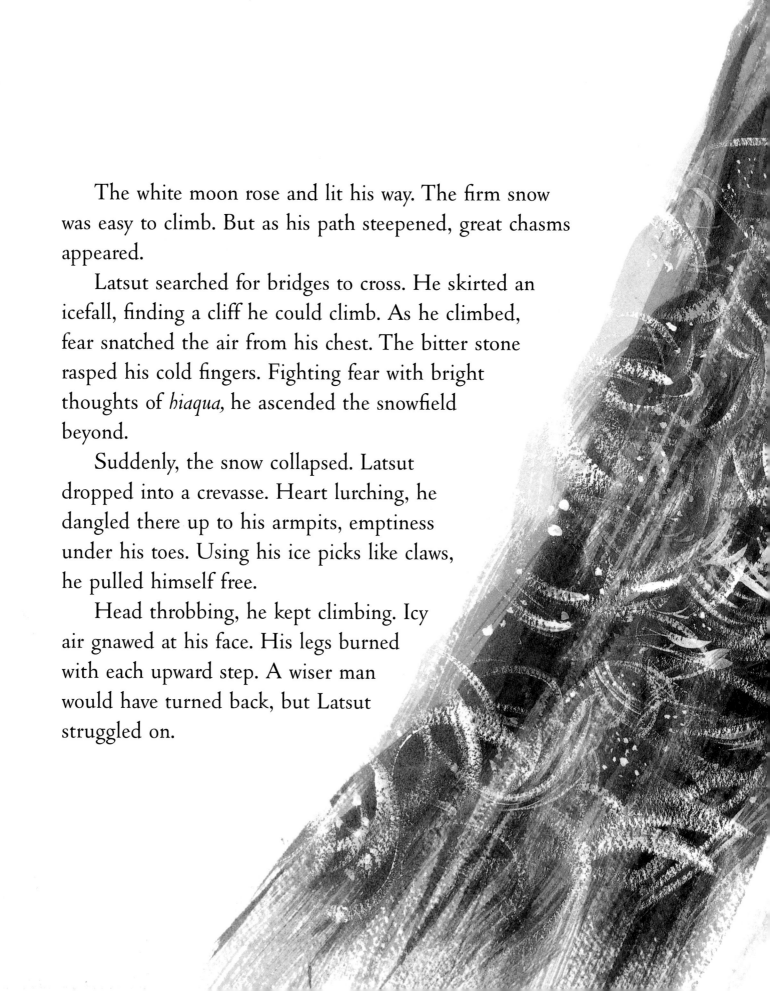

The white moon rose and lit his way. The firm snow was easy to climb. But as his path steepened, great chasms appeared.

Latsut searched for bridges to cross. He skirted an icefall, finding a cliff he could climb. As he climbed, fear snatched the air from his chest. The bitter stone rasped his cold fingers. Fighting fear with bright thoughts of *hiaqua,* he ascended the snowfield beyond.

Suddenly, the snow collapsed. Latsut dropped into a crevasse. Heart lurching, he dangled there up to his armpits, emptiness under his toes. Using his ice picks like claws, he pulled himself free.

Head throbbing, he kept climbing. Icy air gnawed at his face. His legs burned with each upward step. A wiser man would have turned back, but Latsut struggled on.

At sunrise, he reached the summit. There in a valley of snow was the lake. Latsut ran and slid to its shore. The dark water trembled. He heard curious sounds, like huge animals breathing. Latsut paid no attention. His gaze was fixed on a tall standing stone, shaped like the head of a salmon.

The first of the signs! thought Latsut.

Beyond stood a stone like a ripe camas bulb.
The miser rushed past it. The last stone was shaped
like the head of an elk. He knelt at its base and dug
into the snow.

When his pick scraped the snow, he heard
a loud *swoof!* Latsut spun around.

An enormous otter slid out of the lake. It was almost as large as a man. Behind it came twelve more huge otters. They formed a wide circle around him and watched every motion.

Latsut was uneasy, but still he kept digging, determined to find the *hiaqua*. The otters thumped their tails upon the snow.

The miser dug through snow and rock. When he set down his ice pick to rest, the largest otter struck him with its tail.

Each of the others struck him in turn, knocking him sprawling. A sensible man would have fled. Latsut simply groped for his ice pick. The otters retreated.

Determined, the miser kept digging. The otters kept thumping the snow. They circled around him, closer and closer, until he could feel their warm breath.

He moved a piece of rock so thin it crumbled in his fingers. Beneath was a cavity filled with *hiaqua*. He thrust in his arms up to his shoulders. There was no bottom, no end to this treasure!

He pulled out long strings of the precious *hiaqua*. He wrapped four strings around his waist, draped three strings of shells on each shoulder, and clutched five more strings in each hand. Staggering to his feet, he knew he could carry no more. *I will return,* thought Latsut, *for more treasure.*

He waddled away, a man with no manners. He offered no gift to the mountain. He left nothing to thank his own totem.

The spirits awoke in a rage. The otters beat a warning
with their tails. A cloud boiled up out of the lake, dark with
the anger of spirits.

I must hurry! thought Latsut.

As he descended, the cloud spilled out over the mountain.
An icy wind howled all around him. Latsut clung to his treasure.

I found it, he thought. *This hiaqua is mine!*

Ha, ha, hiaqua! jeered the spirit of the wind, hurling Latsut
into a snowbank.

Struggling free, Latsut tossed five strings in its face.
"Take these, but you'll not have the others!"

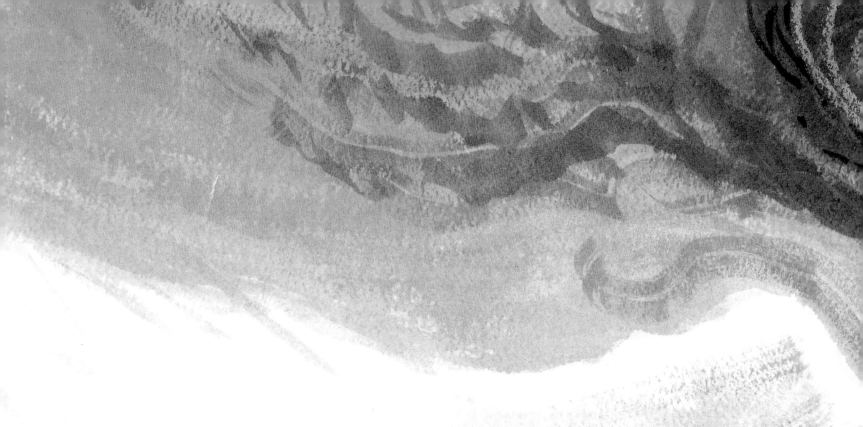

He bounded down the mountain like a goat. His fear of crevasses was nothing compared to his fear of the spirits!

Next he heard the puffing of the otters on his trail. Panicked, he dropped five more strings. The curious otters gave up the chase, stopping to play with the shells.

Latsut hurried on.

Ha, ha, hiaqua! bellowed the spirits of wind, snow, and thunder.

Latsut tried to bargain. "Take three more, but let me keep the rest!" He offered the strings from one shoulder. The spirits were suddenly quiet.

With their next howl, Latsut was thrown over a cliff.
He lay on the snow, bruised and bleeding. *What does this wealth
matter now?* the miser thought, groaning. He shrugged the
hiaqua from his throbbing shoulder. Still groaning, he
got to his feet.

The storm calmed, and it seemed that the spirits
relented. Limping, Latsut crossed the last snowfield
unhindered. He saw the dark shelter of forest below.

Then the ground shook. The whole mountain
roared. *HA, HA, HIAQUA!*

Is wealth more important than life? wondered
Latsut. He dropped to his knees and offered
the shells from his waist. "Take what is
yours, great Ta-co-bet."

With the last of his strength, he
crawled past the edge of the snow.

There he collapsed in deep slumber.

Elk guarded his sleep and built a snug lodge of branches and lichen around him. Snow fell and melted, the seasons turned round, but Latsut slumbered on.

At last a day came when Latsut heard the call of a jay. He crawled out of the lodge and welcomed the morning. To his surprise, his bruises were gone. Where his skin had been torn, he had only faint scars. His long hair was white as the mountain.

Look how the spirits have changed me. I have grown old in the night. He thought of his journey and smiled. *What a fool I have been! And here I sit now, empty-handed.*

Grateful for life, he admired the day. Every stone gleamed in the sunlight. High above floated the mountain. The miser felt rich, although his *hiaqua* was gone.

It is time to return to my family. He started toward home, impatient to see them.

To his amazement, the forest had changed. Huge trees had fallen, blocking the trail. The young trees were taller than he was.

How many seasons have passed while I slept? Latsut did not wait for an answer. He was entranced by the forest. *Such beauty,* he mused. *How precious life is!*

Near sunset the following day, Latsut arrived home. A wealthy old woman sat tending the fire. Although she had changed, Latsut knew her.

"Beca!" he cried. "What has happened?"

"Old man, I am glad you are home. Sit down beside me and have some boiled salmon."

As he ate, Beca explained. "You have been gone many years. Our children are grown now and have their own children. Yet all of these years I have waited, certain that you would return."

"What a treasure you are!" said Latsut. He was glad she had waited so long. And he was ashamed. He had left her to care for their children alone. He wept for the years he had lost in his quest for *hiaqua.*

In autumn, Latsut gave a feast for the tribe. He told them the tale of his journey.

"Ta-co-bet has taught me the meaning of wealth. It is here in the elk and the deer, in the laughter of children. It is here in the salmon and cedar. Wealth is the warmth of the fire, the water that quenches my thirst. It is the smiles on your faces. Thank you for listening to this old man and accepting his gifts."

Everyone saw how the mountain had changed him. They welcomed him home. Others began to ask his advice, for he had grown wise. And Latsut was content, rich with the love of his people.